Park Stories: *Greenwich Park*

GW00382209

Park Stories: By Force of Will, Alone
© Nicola Barker 2009

ISBN: 978-0-9558761-2-7

Series Editor: Rowan Routh

Published by The Royal Parks
www.royalparks.org.uk

Production by Strange Attractor Press
BM SAP, London, WC1N 3XX, UK
www.strangeattractor.co.uk

Cover design: Ali Hutchinson

Park Stories devised by Rowan Routh

The Royal Parks gratefully acknowledges the financial support of Arts Council England.

Printed by Kennet Print, Devizes, UK on 100% post-consumer recycled Cyclus offset paper using vegetable-based inks.

By Force of Will, Alone

Nicola Barker

THE
ROYAL
PARKS

By Force of Will, Alone

His given name was Sydney Figge, and he liked to call
himself 'an open book' (although the type of book he might
be – or aspire to be – Figge never, strictly specified; perhaps
a battered, ring-bound notepad, empty but for a stray,
suspiciously pubic-looking silver hair, a bloody thumb-print
and a squashed moth; or an ancient, crumbling volume
of obscene, Icelandic limericks – un-translated; or a badly
water-stained technical manual – circa 1956 – detailing the
basic maintenance procedures of a now-utterly-obsolete
swimming-pool pump).

Figge was, in short (and as the local, Greenwich
Constabulary would happily attest), anything but open –
quite the contrary, in fact. While he was resolutely jovial (i.e.
invariably plastered) and rarely, if ever, taciturn (he could
cheerfully talk the back- end off the Proverbial Ass), Figge
was also profoundly – almost heroically – evasive by nature.

His mother – an asphyxiatingly righteous, flame-
haired, Protestant widow (late of Tulse Hill), who wore
knee-high socks, flat shoes and skirts manufactured from the
kind of tweed solely engineered to graze a child's cheek –
had been blessed with a mesmerisingly huge pair of hands:
'ham hands', her chapped, pink palms reeking of carbolic,
her slap directly equivalent in both force and impact to that
of the flat of an oiled cricket bat.

She was also celebrated for her prodigious chin
(a smooth, fleshy baton which could effortlessly direct the
thinking of an entire Church Hall by merely rising or falling
by a couple of centimetres) and a fearful glower (that could
instantly hush a squeaky pram wheel – at forty feet – as it
innocently trundled past her).

Sydney was her fifth child (the only boy, and the youngest). He had been named, on a whim, after a character in her second favourite book; *A Tale of Two Cities*. (The Bible, quite predictably, being her first: her daughters were a heady cocktail of Miriams, Marys and Marthas).

Figge had never read the novel (or any novel, for that matter – he was profoundly dyslexic), but he took a casual pride in his literary forebear, Sydney Carton, the tragically dissolute but unswervingly loyal and lovelorn legal assistant who sacrificed his life on the scaffold to save · another ('It is a far, far better thing that I do, than I have ever done,' etc).

Figge's literary predecessor had started off badly but had gradually come good. Figge, however, had no aspirations to moral or spiritual improvement, preferring to inhabit Dickens' character in his earlier, rather more liberal and intemperate mode e.g. as 'a dissipated cat,' 'an insensible dog', 'an amazingly good jackal,' 'devilish,' 'ill-conditioned,' 'an unornamental piece of furniture...' etc.

There was certainly no denying that Figge was a man of prodigious appetites: his bleary gaze and uniformly high colour signified as much. His trademark toddle (brought on by gout) was another strong indicator. Figge could walk great distances for a man of his age (fifty-seven) and habits (uniformly bad), but invariably resembled a creature struggling – against all the odds – to remain upright, in a high wind, on a treacherous bridge fashioned entirely from rope.

Insofar as he was tender – a word which he'd much rather apply to his steak (which he liked raw) than his emotions (which he liked vulcanized) – he directed his affections towards animals, who, in his extensive experience, were generally more obliging than people and definitely less prone to disappoint.

Figge would rarely be seen out on his constant

perambulations (around Deptford, where he lived, Greenwich, which he liked to colonize, and its Royal Park, his spiritual fiefdom) without his shadowy companion, Lindy, an ancient, one-eyed, sheepdog bitch who always carried a small scrap of kitchen lino with her (for play, and for comfort), which she gaily offered up to strangers ('Go on! Take it! It's yours!') and then hotly defended ('WAH!') with all the sudden, unbidden ferocity of a wolverine newly-delivered of a hairless pup.

Whether open or shut (and let's not – Please God – quibble about it here), there were, nevertheless, many fascinating things to discover about Sydney Figge (his time spent as a whaler with the Japanese fleet, for starters; the existence of three illegitimate sons – one mute, one an albino, the third a successful city broker; his amazing proficiency at the Argentine tango; his double-jointed tongue...) but perhaps the most significant of all these (in relation to this current tale, at least) was Sydney Figge's unlikely procurement of the honourable title of Greenwich's Mayor.

One small fly in the ointment: Greenwich already had a Mayor, a capital chap – benevolent in spirit, charitable in inclination, an all-round good egg – called Barney Barnwell-Clarke, who laboured under the illusion of having taken on this elevated role himself (by dint of being formally elected to it).

But Sydney Figge didn't allow this niggling detail to worry him unduly, he was far too busy *being* mayor to allow himself this luxury. Instead he gamely endeavoured to integrate his mayoral duties (such as he perceived them) into his – admittedly, somewhat limited – employment portfolio ('it is, after all' – he was often wont to mutter – 'chiefly a ceremonial gig').

Figge's Mayoral obligations centred on the Royal Park (where he liked to spend a significant percentage of his days) and included:

1) Standing outside the Royal Observatory and helpfully advising tourists ('It's free to get in, but – trust me – you'll be wasting your time. There's nothing worth looking at in there, just a load of old tat and telescopes... Although if you happen to be *interested* in old tat and telescopes, then by all means...' [*roll of eyes, dismissive wave of hand*], 'be my guest').

2) Acting as a spontaneous referee at the tennis courts ('Oi! You! In the yellow skirt! That ball was out. Your backhand's all over the shop. Get a grip on yourself...' [*takes quick swig of beer*], '...And you...Yes, you, with the ridiculous fringe: do your bloody laces up.')

3) Lying on his back in the empty fountain outside the Old Royal Naval College (currently operating as a school of music) and conducting (with a couple of disposable straws) as students held recitals inside. Sometimes shouting out requests ('Do *Delilah*! Do *Dirty Old Town*! Do something by The Chieftains! Hey! *Hey*! Why not pull your heads out of your arses and play something we all actually *know*, for once, eh?').

4) 'Publicising' The Honest Sausage (his favourite food stall in the park) by lounging around outside and conversing with customers until offered a free sample as an incentive to move away ('*Nah*! You don't want to go to the Tea Rooms, love. It's horribly claustrophobic. I went in there once and my cup melted. A china cup! I swear to God, it just melted in my hands. Then, when I went to the counter and started making a fuss – which *anybody* would – they called in the police. Got me banged up in a nut house for a month... [*pauses. Listens to the distant sound of a fire engine*] Isn't it funny how you only ever hear fire sirens when it's threatening to rain? [*Glances up into the sky, scowling*] Wouldn't squirrels look so much better with wings? Think about it... With wings and with feathers and with a neat, little beak. A *thick* beak – like a finch's beak. *Think* about it. *Seriously*. Don't walk off...

Why's she walking off?').
5) Organising groups of young boys into small gangs to collect twigs and broken branches in the park's flower beds and borders which could then be sold on for firewood (by the gate leading out to the Roman Remains) so that the proceeds might be distributed among local 'worthy causes'.
6) Offering to pose – for a small gratuity – with wedding parties by the park's scenic lake ('Yes, I *know* I said she *doesn't* bite, because she doesn't bite. She only bites if you mess with her lino. She loves that lino. You'd have to be a fool to try and take it off her... [*long pause*] Is it deep?').
7) Policing the use of Frisbees in the park ('They're banned in the park. Everybody knows that. No, I won't give it back. Oh really? *Really*?! Well then try and make me, Guv'. Go on. Go *on*. Try and make me.')
8) When things were especially 'slow' on his patch, Figge liked to cause a commotion by introducing the general public to the ancient art of 'tumbling.' This reckless pursuit had traditionally taken place on the steep hill to the north of the Observatory, directly below the statue of General James Wolfe.

Figge had personalised this activity, and liked to call his own, idiosyncratic performance of it (i.e. a dramatic, drunken, apparently 'accidental' cartwheel, turning into an inordinately ungainly high-speed topple, culminating in a sudden, crashing, howling sprawl) 'The Figge Roll'.

He had been respectfully asked (by the Head Park-Keeper and the police) to discontinue this practice after twice colliding with picnickers (in one instance breaking a woman's nose – and fracturing his own collarbone). A fence had even been built to enclose the offending area in a desperate attempt to prevent further anti-social infractions from taking place.

It should possibly be noted at this point (which seems as good a point as any other), that while Figge naturally relished the considerable local status that being Mayor afforded him, he still cheerfully maintained that this lofty endowment had never been actively sought on his part ('I don't have an ambitious bone in my body – never have had. I just take each day as it comes...'), but that it had been pressed upon him, unexpectedly, by The Fates.

Of course there were others (and Barnwell-Clarke was undisputedly one) who felt that Figge had acquired this prestigious nomenclature not by random happen-chance or fluke or luck, but by force of will, alone.

Whatever your take on it, there was certainly no denying that the start of Figge's phantom Mayoral reign had been a signally unpropitious one. In order to supplement his meagre disability allowance (Sydney always hotly maintained that 'disability is a state of the mind, not of the body' – a platitude which, in his own case, was 100% accurate) he would sometimes help out an old friend – a pugnacious coke-head called Timothy Farrow (who wore one of South London's most convincing toupées – as Figge never tired of telling people) with his bric-a-brac stall on Greenwich Market.

Figge was not – this may surprise you – an especially reliable employee (the lure of the snug at The Spanish Galleon was often extremely powerful) and on one, notable occasion, after stashing three litre bottles of Pink Lady under the stall and partaking of them, copiously, throughout the day, he fell into a drunken stupor during the afternoon lull and managed to part company with the entire contents of Farrow's cashbox (not to mention several of his most treasured wares, including an exquisitely stuffed guinea fowl).

When Figge did finally awaken, it was after dark, and he found himself strapped to a broken chair in an empty car park (the stalls had long-since been cleared), wearing a paste tiara, clip-on earrings and a magnificent assortment of fancy, faux gold chains (including a huge Saint Christopher – so big it might almost be thought to *hinder* travel – a horn of plenty and a dolphin with a crystal heart clumsily etched into its gaudy tail).

A man has his pride. To prove to an exultant Farrow that he had not been one-upped, Figge proceeded to wear these low-grade adornments for several days. The tiara was eventually broken in a scuffle outside the deer enclosure, when Sam 'Winky' Stevens (a mainstay of The Friends of Greenwich Park and an aspirant water-colourist of no perceptible talent) refused to relinquish Syd's favourite bench because he was 'making a painting' in that particular spot.

One earring was lost during the annual collection of horse-chestnuts (an illegal operation which Syd generally undertook, at dusk, with the aid of his old mucker, local restaurateur, Wang Cho). Yet the chains somehow – almost miraculously – remained *in situ*.

People liked them and would often comment on them, with a smile. Some even went so far as to add to the collection. Nico Hodges (who busked with his accordion by the park gates most weekends) had contributed several which he'd acquired from his daughter, after her boyfriend (an aspirant rapper; MC Botox) had upgraded his low-grade bling to the real thing.

A girl called Tabitha (an imaginative Goth who reeked of cardomom oil and worked, part-time, in the park's Wildlife Centre) took special delight in fashioning Syd a series of baroque creations from a consignment of old, brass cinema fitments which her father, a builder, had randomly discovered in a lock-up in Foots Hill.

As the volume of Figge's chest decor expanded, so too did his air of casual hauteur, and it didn't take long before the satirical tag of 'Greenwich's Mayor' was being fondly applied by all who came across him.

Thomas George (who sold traditional, home-made ice-cream from a little copper barrel which he wheeled – illicitly – around the park) cheerfully contributed a slightly-battered, three-cornered hat to Figge's imposing 'look' (after his brother graced the chorus in an amateur production of *The Pirates of Penzance*). A smart frock coat was subsequently snaffled after it was briefly abandoned on the bandstand (during a toilet break) by a visiting trombonist from Ayr.

With the acquisition of said coat, Figge's Mayoral demeanour might finally be said to have been rendered complete, but it was a chance encounter during a Sunday morning 'Fungus Foray' (ten months later) that was to both shape – and cement – Figge's ever-tightening stranglehold on Greenwich's fragile social and political economy.

Bradley Monk was a retired ear, nose and throat specialist with a passion for claret, a peerless collection of eighteenth century French decanters and a seething grudge against his next-door-neighbour. His neighbour was a man of fine character who had allowed his wife – in a moment of weakness – to plant a Monkey Puzzle tree three metres from the fence that divided their property.

While Monk never referred to the matter publicly, over time he grew convinced that it was the toxic resin from said tree that had finally put paid to some of the finest bushes in his beloved, traditional English scented rose border (he was wrong. The real reason, as it happens, was a Magnesium deficiency).

On espying the unabashed Figge casually relieving himself inside the protective shelter of the low skirts of a Scotch Pine that fine, Sunday morn (while hunting for a *Gomphidius rutilus* – an edible mushroom which turns black when stewed in vinegar), Bradley Monk had – it would seem – discovered the answer to all his prayers.

12

After a little, innocent investigation on the
internet, Monk (who – rather auspiciously – was always
more than ready to provide the thirsty Figge with a can or
three of creamy stout) was soon able to drop subtle hints
to his suggestible quarry about Barnwell-Clarke's official
movements (i.e. a fireworks party in the park, the opening
of a new science lab in a nearby school, the awarding of
a medal for a random act of bravery). Before long Figge
suddenly began (he knew not why) to feel a powerful –
almost uncontrollable – urge to turn up at these events
himself ('Just to... *ahem*... put myself about a bit').

Barnwell-Clarke was, at root (hyphen or no), a
fundamentally humble and well-meaning soul. He tried his
best to be the bigger man and to take Figge's gate-crashing
in his stride (although it never failed to astonish him how
tolerantly the British public generally responded to a
patently drunken stranger arriving, uninvited, at one of their
events, making short work of the buffet and then loudly
reciting the first twenty-three stanzas of the *Rubaiyat of
Omar Khayyam*).

Of course Barnwell-Clarke would've been a saint
not to have felt marginally belittled by what he (quite
rightly) perceived to be Figge's cheerful satire of both
himself and the venerable office he represented (not to
mention the public's tacit cooperation – nay encouragement
– of Figge in his dastardly pursuit).

And so it was for the sake of this office (he
dogmatically maintained) that he eventually felt compelled
to take action (the final straw came after Barnwell-Clarke
was five minutes late to start a sponsored dog walk – he'd
pierced his left eye on a Monkey Puzzle branch while raking
up leaves in his garden. Figge – who was on time – had
opened the event himself with a quick toot on a pink plastic
toy trumpet and a little jig, followed – when people began to
lose interest and move off – by some rather choice language

and a bungled attempt to moon a Conservative councillor).

After consulting with a lawyer, it was decided that while it was impossible to stop Figge from impersonating the Mayor on Greenwich's streets, the park itself – because it was still subject to an infinite spectrum of antiquated Royal by-laws and regulations – might offer Barnwell-Clarke a glimmer of hope.

A meeting of interested parties was duly called (and held at the Pavilion Tea Rooms – a place Figge violently eschewed).

There was an impressive turn out. Sam 'Winky' Stevens initially held sway for the nays (and as a representative of The Friends his opinions had considerable weight). He was quickly followed by a tearful member of the Marathon Mums (a park-based, post-natal fitness group) who Figge had once idly nick-named 'Jelly-tits.'

Several irate Frisbee-players also vented their spleen (which was extensive), followed by five brides, a cluster of 'concerned parents', three violinists (from the music school) and two representatives of the Royal Observatory, one of whom – quite inadvertently – dealt Figge's cause what might easily have been a shattering blow.

'We have this rule,' he mused, 'which strictly prohibits public performances in the vicinity of the Observatory...'

'Well, given that Figge isn't *actually* Mayor,' Jelly-tits interrupted him, excitedly, 'Doesn't that mean he's just "performing" the role, and, as such, could be legitimately excluded on those grounds?'

After a further period of excitable negotiation, Barnwell-Clarke (who was chairing the meeting) noticed a couple of uneasy-looking individuals perched at a corner table. He cleared his throat.

'Perhaps there may be parties here present,' he suggested, glancing over at them, encouragingly, 'who might wish to speak in *favour* of Mr Figge?'

Nico Hodges slowly stood up. 'I was almost robbed by a couple of young hoodlums while I was out busking, once,' he muttered, 'And if Syd hadn't happened along...' he shrugged, 'Who knows? As it was, he chased those little shits all the way down to the Cutty Sark.'

Then Tabitha rose to her feet. 'I fell off my bike on the way to work and dislocated my shoulder. I was in agony. Syd just turned up, grabbed me by the arm, and popped it straight back in again.'

'Anyone else?' Barnwell-Clarke surveyed the room, tremulously.

Jelly-tits bounced up again. 'He did actually advise me to wear two bras,' she sniffed, 'Initially I just thought he was being facetious, but I tried it the next day and I actually found the extra support invaluable...'

'I'd suffered from a fair amount of back pain over the years,' a Frisbee-player interrupted, 'And after Figge confiscated my Frisbee, I realised what a harmful effect the game was having on my neck.'

The second Observatory representative stood up, 'I must admit,' she confessed, 'that we often find Figge's disparaging remarks about the Observatory very useful in the Summer months for keeping visitor numbers down to a manageable level.'

A bride sprang to her feet, 'He called some wild parrots down from the trees with these really manky bits of cut apple. One sat on my hand. It was my favourite wedding photo.'

'I gave up using watercolours and switched to acrylics,' Sam 'Winky' Stevens suddenly blurted out, 'And I've recently done some of the best work in my artistic career.'

'Right. Good...'

Barnwell-Clarke mournfully appraised the packed Tea Rooms for a while, 'Well I think I've probably heard enough...'

He drew a deep breath: 'Meeting adjourned!'

And so it was that Sydney Figge was saved (but not for long, alas). Three weeks later (to the hour), after consuming an entire bottle of Amarula, Figge – in a moment of irresponsible *bonhomie* – bounced over the fence by the statue of General James Wolfe, and commenced tumbling his way down the hill (to the evocative soundtrack of the gasps of an awed crowd).

Some time later, as the ambulance-men strapped his lifeless body onto a stretcher, one peered up, frowning, at the other; 'The little, pointed, gold charm that pierced his wind-pipe...' he muttered, 'I've never seen one before. What is it, exactly?'

'It's a Horn of Plenty,' the other responded, 'A symbol of female fertility. Some call it the 'Harvest cone'. It goes back to the story of Almalthea, the mythological goat. She fed Zeus on her breast milk. Once, while they were playing together, Zeus accidentally snapped off her horn and changed her into a unicorn. To pay her back, he then returned her horn to her, and with it, the power to give the person in possession of it anything they wished for.'

'Do you think he wished for *this*?' the first ambulance-man wondered, nodding towards Figge's corpse, wryly.

The second ambulance-man didn't answer at first. An old, one-eyed sheepdog had just placed a tattered piece of lino at his feet and was now gazing up at him, imploringly.

'D'you want to play, old girl?'

He slowly leaned down, his tired face suddenly lighting up with a tender smile, and then reached out a tentative hand towards it.